BABAR
and the GHOST

LAURENT DE BRUNHOFF

A RANDOM HOUSE BOOK

It was a perfect day for a hike. King Babar and Queen Celeste got the family's backpacks and they set off with the children, Pom, Flora, and Alexander. Soon Cornelius and the Old Lady wanted to rest. "Babar promised that we would go all the way to the Black Castle," said cousin Arthur. "We have plenty of time," said the Old Lady, and she stretched out her legs.

Just as they came to the Black Castle, a storm broke out. The sky grew dark and the wind began to howl. Big drops of rain started to fall. Arthur ran up ahead. "Let's go into the castle and get out of the rain," he said.

Cornelius shook his head. "No, that is a terrible idea," he said. "That castle looks haunted." Babar laughed. "Surely you don't believe in ghosts, Cornelius! Come on. Haunted or not, let's go in."

They walked down the castle's long hall. Suddenly Arthur saw a white shape! It came and went so fast that Arthur wondered if he really saw it.

Babar quickly built a big fire and they began to dry off. "Will it never stop raining?" sighed the Old Lady. "Oh dear!" whined Cornelius, who hated mice and spiders. Arthur said nothing about the white shape. He didn't want to frighten Cornelius.

It did not stop raining, and Babar and Celeste decided they would spend the night in the castle. "Hurray!" cried the children. "Now we can go exploring!" They ran through the empty castle, down dark corridors, over squeaking and creaking floors. "A ghost! A ghost!" they whined, trying to sound like Cornelius.

While chasing each other and laughing, they bumped into a big suit of armor. It fell over with a loud crash. They stopped laughing when the suit of armor began to move! It sat up, it lifted its helmet, and a ghost poked his head out. *A real ghost!*

Without a sound, the ghost rose out of the heavy suit of armor.

With a noisy clatter, the terrified children fled up the big staircase.

They rushed up to Babar and Celeste. Their hearts pounded as they told about the ghost. "I warned you this castle is haunted!" grumbled Cornelius. Babar calmed everyone. "Come, come," he said. "There is no such thing as a ghost. Now we must sleep. We've had a long day. We will all sleep together in this room. And we'll go back to Celesteville early tomorrow."

Babar, Celeste, and the Old Lady fell asleep right away. Soon Cornelius was asleep, too. But not the children. They were too excited. "Why don't we try to find the ghost again?" whispered Arthur. "Do you think that is a good idea?" asked Alexander. "Let's go," said Flora, and they all crept silently out to the hallway.

The children wandered from room to room. Suddenly they heard a very deep voice. "Good evening. I am Baron Bardula." The ghost was behind them! "This is a painting of me as a brave knight long, long ago." Then he disappeared and in a moment returned, walking right through the wall. What a good trick!

The baron was a friendly ghost. He showed the children around his castle and told them of battles and adventures of long ago. Pom pleaded, "Oh, you must come with us to Celesteville." "Well, yes, that might be good fun," said the ghost with a little smile. "It is so quiet here."

Early the next morning they all started back to Celeste-ville. "Why are the children lagging behind so?" wondered Babar. "They usually run ahead of us." Cornelius was happy to get away from that castle. If he only knew that the ghost was following them home!

Everyone in Celesteville greeted them with questions: "Where were you during the storm?" "What did you do all night?" Arthur ran to his friend Zephir the monkey. "Just wait, and I'll tell you everything!" he whispered.

Arthur told Zephir about the ghost and his tricks.
"Only we children can see him! What fun we can have!"
said Arthur. And, indeed, funny things began to happen.
The Old Lady and Celeste were drinking lemonade in the
garden. Slowly the pitcher rose in the air and filled their
glasses. "Did you see that!" they cried.

Arthur and Babar were planting flowers, when suddenly they heard the lawn mower. It was running all by itself! Putt, putt, putt, it went, right through the flowers. Arthur burst out laughing. "I don't think that is funny," said Babar angrily. "Your friend Zephir started the mower, didn't he?" Arthur giggled. "No he didn't," he said.

While Cornelius was reading in the study, he felt someone snatch his eyeglasses. He dropped his book and jumped up in surprise. "Someone stole my glasses," he complained to Babar. "Did you do it, Alexander?" asked Babar. "Not me!" said Alexander.

After dinner Babar and Celeste were happily playing music with Arthur and the Old Lady. Suddenly there was a loud, sour squawk from the saxophone! "Who did that?" shouted Babar. Arthur laughed. He knew!

The next day, the ghost had a good time pushing Alexander through the park in a shopping cart.

But the ghost's favorite game was hide-and-seek. The children chased him, knocking over chairs and calling, "Baron, Baron, where are you?" There he was—then he disappeared. They finally found him in a chest of drawers, all neatly folded like a sheet. The children choked with laughter. Just then, the door flew open. "What's all this racket about?" asked Babar.

Babar was wondering how to put an end to these strange happenings when suddenly horns began honking, tires screeched, and everyone began shouting angrily.

A blue car was racing through all the traffic. Babar couldn't believe his eyes. The car had no driver!

The police—along with Babar, Zephir, and Arthur—took off after the blue car. But the driverless blue car was too fast. Then Babar got a message on his radio headset. The principal of the school couldn't control his students. "The children refuse to leave the playground. They are pretending to play with a ghost. Of course, there is no ghost," said the principal. Babar frowned. "Let's hurry to the school," he said. "We must find out once and for all what's going on."

In the school playground the children were shouting, "The ghost! See the ghost!" Babar saw no ghost. But he said, "Ghost, if you are there, listen to me. This can't go on. You are turning everything topsy-turvy in Celesteville. Go back to your castle." But Bardula did not answer. Babar was very upset.

That evening when the moon appeared, Bardula told the children that he was going home. "I had a wonderful time, thanks to you, but I must admit that this lively life is tiring me out." The children waved good-bye and begged him to return. "I shall, my friends, I shall," said the ghost as he faded into the night sky.